W9-BWJ-507

My 1st Classic Story

Sleeping Beauty

a retelling of the Grimm's fairy tale

by Eric Blair

illustrated by Todd Ouren

PICTURE WINDOW BOOKS
a capstone imprint

My First Classic Story is published by Picture Window Books
A Capstone Imprint
151 Good Counsel Drive, P.O. Box 669
Mankato, Minnesota 56002
www.capstonepub.com

Library of Congress Cataloging-in-Publication Data
Blair, Eric.
Sleeping Beauty : a retelling of the Grimms' fairy tale
retold by Eric Blair ; illustrated by Todd Ouren.
p. cm. -— (My first classic story)
Summary: Enraged at not being invited to the
princess's christening, a wicked fairy casts a spell that
dooms the princess to sleep for one hundred years.
ISBN 978-1-4048-6080-3 (library binding)
[1. Fairy tales. 2. Folklore—Germany.] I. Ouren, Todd, ill.
II. Grimm, Jacob, 1785-1863. III. Grimm, Wilhelm, 1786-1859.
IV. Sleeping Beauty. English. V. Title.
PZ8.B5688Sle 2011
398.2—dc22
[E]   2010003620

Art Director: Kay Fraser
Graphic Designer: Emily Harris

The story of *Sleeping Beauty* has been passed down for generations. There are many versions of the story. The following tale is a retelling of the original version. While the story has been cut for length and level, the basic elements of the classic tale remain.

Once upon a time, there lived a king and a queen.

"Oh, how I wish we had a child," the king said.

The next year, the queen had a baby girl.
Everyone called her Beauty.

The king threw a big party. He invited everyone except the bad fairy.

The twelve good fairies each gave
Beauty a gift.

"You will be the most beautiful
princess in the world," said one.

"You will be the smartest princess in the world," said another.

The fairies gave the princess gift after gift.

Suddenly, the bad fairy showed up. She was very angry. She put a spell on Beauty.

"When Beauty is fifteen years old, she will prick her finger with a spindle and die." With that, the bad fairy left.

One fairy had not given a gift to Beauty yet.

"I cannot break the spell," the fairy said.
"But I can change it. Beauty will not die.
She will sleep. After 100 years, a prince
will come and break the spell."

The king had all the spindles in the kingdom burned.

Beauty grew up with all the fairies' gifts.
Everyone loved her.

One day, when she was fifteen years old, Beauty was alone in the palace. She went to the tower. At the top, she found an old woman. The old woman was really the bad fairy.

"What are you doing?" asked Beauty.

"I am spinning," said the old woman.
"Would you like to try?"

Beauty touched the spindle. It pricked
her finger. She fell into a deep sleep.

So did the entire palace.

Large thorns grew around the palace. Many
princes tried to enter, but nobody succeeded.

One hundred years passed. A brave prince came to the palace.

"I am not afraid," the prince told an old man.

"I will save the princess," he said.

He stood near the thorns. They became
beautiful flowers.

The prince ran into the palace. Everyone
was sleeping.

Then he ran to the tower.

The moment he saw Beauty, he fell in love.

28

He kissed her. The spell was broken.

Beauty woke up. So did the rest of the palace.

"I have been waiting for you for a very long time," she said.

Beauty and the prince were married that
day. And they lived happily ever after.

The End